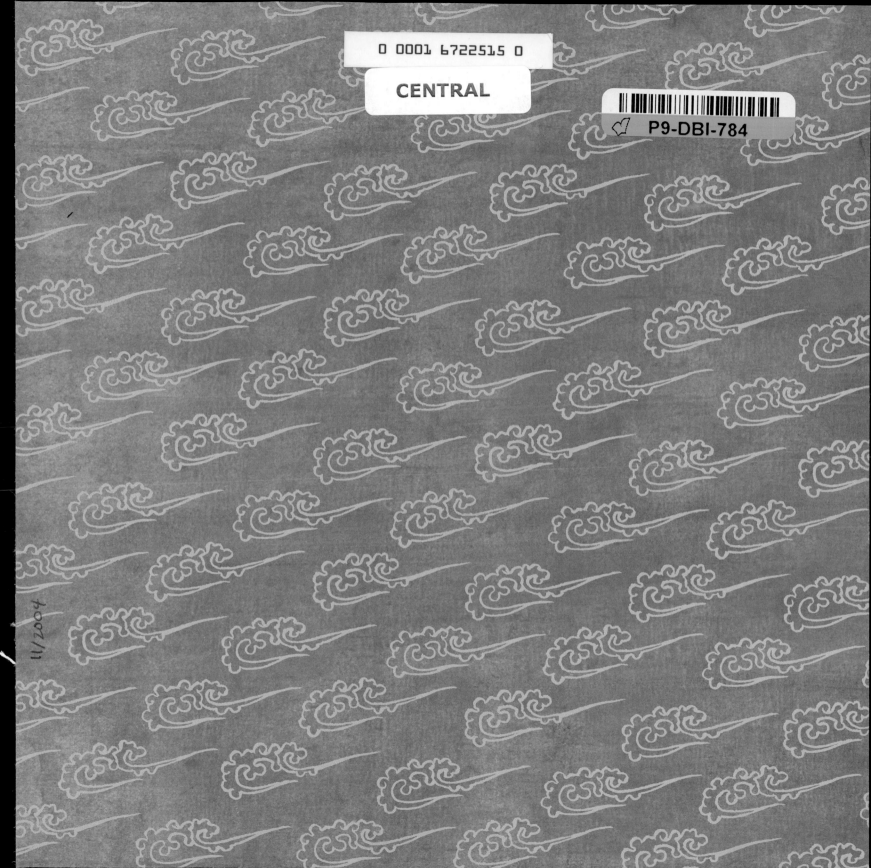

11/2004

Korean Children's Favorite Stories

Korean Children's Favorite Stories

Retold by Kim So-un

Illustrated by Jeong Kyoung-Sim

TUTTLE PUBLISHING
Boston • Rutland, Vermont • Tokyo

As seen in the first story in this collection of stories for children, "The Story Bag," stories do not like to be hoarded, but want to be told and told again, passing always from lip to lip. I have chosen and retold here a number of Korean folk tales that have been handed down by word of mouth from one generation to the next. There are stories that have been told by grandparents to their grandchildren, huddled on the heated floors of Korean homes in the dead of winter, with the cold snow-laden winds raging outside. There are stories repeated in the yards of Korean homes to children seated on straw mats in the cool of a summer evening, smoke from mosquito coils whirling about their faces. These are short tales recounted in great merriment by farming folk, as they rest from their work in the fields in the shade of a nearby tree. These are stories which the Korean children of countless generations have wept and laughed over. They reveal the inevitable foibles of people everywhere and expose the human-like qualities of animals and the animal-like qualities of humans. In these stories ants talk, a baby rabbit outwits a tiger, a tree fathers a child, and a toad saves a whole village. They reflect the serenity of the men and women nurtured by the ancient land of Korea. Here may be found stories which echo those told in many countries throughout the world. Here are also stories that are peculiar to Korea. These stories were first heard in my childhood in Korea. I hope they will use their magic powers to rise above all language barriers and speak directly to the hearts of all "children" between the ages of eight and eighty in other lands.

Author—Kim So-un

Published by Tuttle Publishing,
an imprint of Periplus Editions (HK) Ltd
with editorial offices at 153 Milk Street,
Boston, Massachusetts 02109
and 130 Joo Seng Road,
#06-01, Singapore 368357

First Edition, January 1955
Illustrations © 2004 Jeong Kyoung-Sim

LCC Card No. 2003112851
ISBN 0-8048-3591-8
Printed in Singapore
First printing, 2004

09 08 07 06 05 04
6 5 4 3 2 1

Distributed by:

North America, Latin America and Europe
Tuttle Publishing, 364 Innovation Drive,
North Clarendon, VT 05759-9436.
Tel (802) 773 8930, Fax (802) 773 6993
Email: info@tuttlepublishing.com
Website: www.tuttlepublishing.com

Asia Pacific
Berkeley Books Pte Ltd, 130 Joo Seng Road,
#06–01/03, Olivine Building, Singapore 368357.
Tel (65) 6280 1330, Fax (65) 6280 6290
Email: inquiries@periplus.com.sg

Japan
Tuttle Publishing, Yaekari Building, 3F 5-4-12, Osaki,
Shinagawa-ku, Tokyo, Japan 141-0032
Tel (03) 5437 0171, Fax (03) 5437 0755
Email: tuttle-sales@gol.com

Indonesia
PT Java Books Indonesia, Jl Kelapa Gading Kirana,
Blok A - 14 No. 17, Jakarta 14240
Tel (62) 21 451 5351, Fax (62) 21 453 4987
Email: cs@javabooks.co.id

Contents

The Story Bag

There once lived a very rich family. They had only one child, a boy, who loved to have stories told to him. Whenever he met a new person, he would say, "Tell me another different story." And each time he would store away the story he heard in a small bag he carried at his belt. So many stories did he hear that soon the bag was packed tight and he had to push hard to get each new story in. Then, to make sure that none of the stories escaped, he kept the bag tied tightly at the mouth.

The boy eventually grew into a handsome young man. The time came for him to take a wife. A bride was chosen for him, and the whole house was preparing to greet the young master's new wife. Everything was in an uproar.

9

Now, there happened to be in this rich home a faithful old servant who had been with the family ever since the time when the story-loving boy was still very young. As the household was preparing for the young master's wedding, this servant was tending a fire on the kitchen hearth. Suddenly his ears caught faint whispering sounds coming from somewhere. He listened carefully and soon discovered that the voices were coming from a bag hanging on the wall. It was the bag of stories which the young master had kept in his childhood. Now it hung forgotten on an old nail on the kitchen wall. The old servant listened carefully.

"Listen everyone," said a voice, "the boy's wedding is to take place tomorrow. He has kept us this long while stuffed in this bag, packed so closely and uncomfortably together. We have suffered for a long time. We must make him pay for this some way or another."

"Yes," said another voice, "I have been thinking the same thing. Tomorrow the young man will leave by horse to bring home his bride. I shall change into bright red berries, ripening by the roadside. There I shall wait for him. I shall be poisonous but shall look so beautiful that he will want to eat me. If he does, I shall kill him."

"And, if he doesn't die after eating the berries," piped up a third voice, "I shall become a clear, bubbling spring by the roadside. I shall have a beautiful gourd dipper floating in me. When he sees me he will feel thirsty and will drink me. When I get inside him, I shall make him suffer terribly."

A fourth voice then broke in. "If you fail, then I shall become an iron skewer, heated red-hot, and I shall hide in the bag of chaff that will be placed by his horse for him to dismount on when he reaches his bride's home. And when he steps on me, I shall burn his feet badly." Because, you see, according to the custom of the land in those days, a bag of chaff was always placed by the bridegroom's horse so that he would not have to step directly on the ground.

Then a fifth voice whispered, "If that fails too, I shall become those poisonous string snakes, thin as threads. Then I shall hide in the bridal chamber. When the bride and the bridegroom have gone to sleep, I shall come out and bite them."

The servant was filled with alarm by what he heard. "This is terrible," he told himself. "I must not let any harm come to the young master. When he leaves the house tomorrow, I must take the bridle and lead his horse myself."

Early next morning, the final preparations were completed, and the wedding procession was ready to set forth. The groom, dressed in his best, came out of the house and mounted his horse. Suddenly the faithful servant came running out and grabbed the horse's bridle. He then asked to be allowed to lead the horse.

The old master of the house said, "You have other work to do. You had better stay behind."

"But I must lead the horse today," the servant said. "I don't care what happens, but I insist that I take the bridle."

He refused to listen to anyone and finally the master, surprised at the old man's obstinacy, allowed him to lead the horse to the bride's home.

As the procession wound along its way, the bridegroom came to an open field. There by the roadside many bright berries were growing. They looked temptingly delicious.

"Wait!" the bridegroom called out. "Stop the horse and pick me some of those big juicy berries."

However, the servant would not stop. In fact, he purposely made the horse hurry on and said, "Oh, those berries. You can find them anywhere. Just be a little patient. I shall pick some for you later." And he gave the horse a good crack of the whip.

After a while, they came to a bubbling spring. Its clear waters seemed cool and tempting. There was even a small gourd dipper floating on the water, as if to invite the passerby to have a drink.

"Bring me some of that water," the bridegroom said to the servant. "I have been thirsty for some time."

But again the servant prodded the horse and hurried by. "Once we get into the shade of those trees, your thirst will soon disappear," he said, and he gave the horse another crack of the whip, a blow much harder than the first one.

The bridegroom grumbled and mumbled from atop his horse. He was in a very bad mood, but the servant took no notice. He only made the horse go faster.

Soon they reached the bride's home. There, already gathered in the yard, was a large crowd of people. The servant led the horse into the compound and stopped it beside the waiting bag of chaff. As the bridegroom put down his foot to dismount, the servant pretended to stumble and shoved the bridegroom to keep him from stepping on the bag.

The bridegroom fell to the straw mats laid out on the ground. He blushed in shame at his clumsy fall. However, he could not scold the servant in front of all the people. So he kept silent and entered the bride's home.

There, the wedding ceremony was held without untoward incident, and the newly married couple returned to the groom's home.

Soon night fell, and the bride and bridegroom retired to their room. The faithful servant armed himself with a

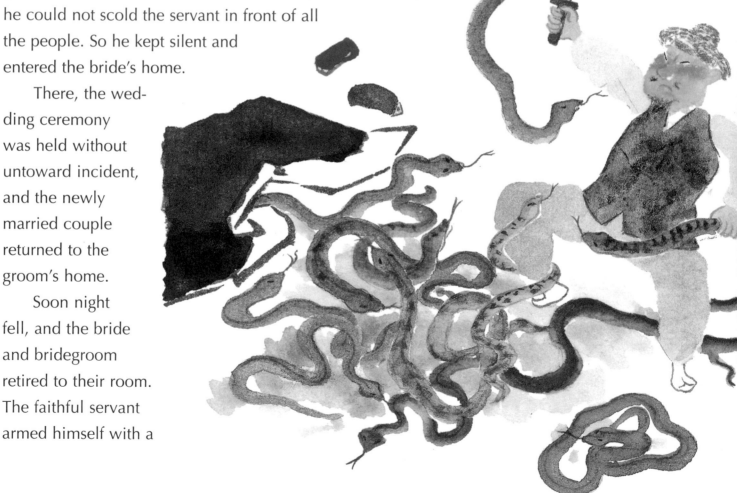

14

sword and hid himself under the veranda outside the bridal chamber. As soon as the bride and bridegroom turned out the lights and went to bed, the servant opened the door of the room and leapt inside.

The newly wed couple were startled beyond description. "Who's there?" they both shouted, jumping out of bed.

"Young master," the servant said, "I shall explain later. Right now, just hurry and get out of the way."

The servant kicked the bedding aside and lifted the mattress. A terrible sight greeted their eyes. There hundreds of string snakes coiled and writhed in a single ball. The servant slashed at the snakes with the sword in his hand. As he cut some into pieces, they opened their red mouths and darted their black forked tongues at him. Other snakes slithered here and there, trying to escape the servant's flashing sword. The servant whirled here and there like a madman and finally killed every one of the snakes in the room.

Then he let out a great sigh of relief and began to say, "Young master, this is the story...." And the old servant recounted all the whispers that he had heard coming from the old bag on the kitchen wall.

That is why when stories are heard they must never be stored away to become mean and spiteful, but must always be shared with other people. In this way, they are passed from one person to another so that as many people as possible can enjoy them.

The Pheasant, the Dove, and the Magpie

There once lived in the same forest a pheasant, a dove, and a magpie. One year the crops failed, and there was nothing for the three of them to eat. "What shall we do? How can we live through this cold winter?" The three talked over their problems and finally decided to call on a mouse who also lived in the same forest. "Surely," they said, "the mouse will have some rice and will share it with us." They decided that the pheasant would go first to see the mouse.

The pheasant was always a proud bird and till then had looked down on the lowly mouse. So, when he came to the home of the mouse, he spoke rudely out of habit.

"Hey there!" the pheasant said haughtily, "where are you? This is the great pheasant. Bring me some food."

Mrs. Mouse was in the kitchen at the back of the house, feeding fuel to her kitchen stove. When she heard the disdainful words of the pheasant, she became very angry. She flew out of the kitchen, a red-hot poker in her hand, and began hitting the pheasant on both his cheeks.

"What's the idea of speaking in such a manner when you have come begging for food. Even if we had rice to throw away, we wouldn't give you any."

Rubbing his red and swollen cheeks, the pheasant ran home in great shame. That is why, to this day, the pheasant's cheeks are red.

Next the dove went to the mouse's home. He, too, was a very proud bird and looked down on the mouse.

"Say, you rice thief! I've come for a bit of food," he said in a rude and haughty manner.

Mrs. Mouse became angry again when she heard the dove speak so rudely. She ran out of her kitchen with a poker in her hand and hit the dove a good blow on the top of his head.

Ever since then, the top of a dove's head has always been blue. It is the bruise that was caused by Mrs. Mouse and her poker.

Lastly, the magpie went to get some food. The magpie knew too well what had happened to his two friends, the pheasant and the dove. He did not want to repeat their mistakes, so he decided to be very, very careful how he spoke.

As soon as he reached the front door of Mr. Mouse's home, he bowed humbly and spoke as politely as possible. "My dear Mr. Mouse," he said, "we have had an extremely poor harvest and I am hungry. Can you not spare me a little food?"

Mr. Mouse came to the front door. "Well, Mr. Magpie, I won't say I shan't give you anything. But aren't you a crony of the pheasant and the dove? If you are, I will certainly have nothing to do with you."

"Oh no, Mr. Mouse," said the magpie, "absolutely not. I've never even heard of them."

"In that case, come in," the mouse said, believing what the magpie told him. The mouse then gave the magpie some rice to take home.

On top of all this, Mrs. Mouse, her good mood restored, said, "Mr. Magpie, you certainly are a refined gentleman. Even your language is different from the rest. You must have had a very good upbringing."

And so, to this day, the magpie is known for his cunning and slyness.

The Bridegroom's Shopping

Away in the country there once lived a long-established family of farmers. There was an only daughter in the family, who had just married. As is the custom in such cases, the bridegroom came to live with his in-laws, for he was to continue the family name.

A few days after the marriage it so happened that the bridegroom had to go to town on some business. As he prepared to leave, his bride asked him, "Will you please buy me a comb in town?"

"Why, of course," he answered, all eager to please his pretty bride.

However, his wife knew that her husband was a very forgetful man. Hadn't both her mother-in-law and father-in-law told her so?

As she was wondering how he could be made to remember, she chanced to look at the sky. There was a new moon, a thin crescent of pale light, shining softly in the sky. It was only three days old, and it looked just like the moon-shaped comb she wanted.

"There," she called to her husband, "look at the moon. Doesn't it look just like a comb? If you forget what you must buy, just remember to look into the sky. The moon will remind you that I want a comb. You will remember, won't you?"

This she repeated again and again, and after she was sure he would remember, she said goodbye to him.

The bridegroom was soon in town. He was so taken up with his business that he completely forgot about his wife's comb. Several days later, his work finished, he packed his belongings and prepared to return home. As he looked around to see if he had forgotten anything, he happened to look out the window, and there he saw a big, round moon shining in the sky. Ten days had passed since he had left home. The moon was no longer a small sliver of light but a round, laughing globe of silver.

The moon suddenly reminded him of his wife's parting words. "Oh, I almost forgot," he told himself. "There was something like the moon I had to buy for my wife. Now, I wonder what it was?"

Try as he might, he could not remember. He knew that it had something to do with the moon—but what? His memory was a blank. "Was it something round like the moon?" he asked himself, "or was it something that shone like the moon?" But not for the life of him could he recall what it was.

"Well," he said at last, "I might as well go to a shop and ask for help."

So the young farmer entered a shop and said, "Good day, Mr. Shopkeeper. Please give me something that looks like the moon, something a woman uses."

The shopkeeper laughed at this strange request. Then he looked around at the goods on his shelf, and his eyes lighted on a small, round hand mirror.

"Oh, I know," the shopkeeper said. "This must be what you want. Look, it's round and looks just like the full moon. You look into it and you can see yourself. A young bride would want it when she pretties herself. I am sure it could be nothing else."

Now, the bridegroom had never seen a mirror before, as they were very rare then. But he thought that surely his wife, the daughter of a rich old farming family, would know what it was. "Yes, this must be what my wife asked me to get," he answered, proud that he could get what his wife wanted.

Soon he was back home in the country again. As soon as he entered the house, his wife asked, "Did you remember to do my shopping for me?"

"Yes," he answered. "Here." And he handed her what he had bought.

The bride, expecting to receive a comb, wondered at the strange round object her husband handed her. She peered into the smooth glass. And what should she see there but the reflection of a young woman and a very pretty woman at that.

"What thing is this!" she cried. "I only asked for a comb, and here you bring home a pretty young woman." The wife turned angrily and ran to her mother.

"Mother, can you imagine anything so silly? I asked my husband to buy me a comb in town, and look what he brought home—a strange young woman!"

"Where? Where is she?" the mother asked, taking the mirror and peering into it.

Of course, the mother saw reflected only the face of a wrinkled old woman. "Why,

my child," she said, "what are you talking about? This must be an old relative of ours from a neighboring village."

"No, you are wrong. It's a young woman," the young wife cried.

"No, it's you who are wrong. Look, she's an old, wrinkled woman," the mother retorted angrily. Thus the two began quarreling.

Just then a small boy came into the room, eating a rice cake. The boy picked up the mirror and peered into it. There he saw another boy eating a rice cake. The boy thought the stranger had taken his.

"Give me back my rice cake," he shouted, "it's mine!" He threw up his hand to strike the boy. The boy in the mirror also raised his arm. The bewildered child, scared by what he saw, began to cry loudly.

The room was filled with din, the two women arguing away at the top of their voices, and the boy crying his head off.

Just then the grandfather passed by and heard the commotion. Wondering what it was all about, he poked his head in the doorway. "What's going on here? What's the matter?" he asked. Then he caught sight of the boy looking at a round object and crying, "Give me back my rice cake!" The grandfather flared with anger to think that someone or something should have taken rice cakes from a small boy.

"Where, where?" he asked. "Show me the thief!" He grabbed the mirror and peered into it. There, staring at him, was a fierce-looking old man, anger written all over his face.

"Why, it's an old man. You ought to be ashamed at your age to jump out and interfere in a quarrel between boys." With these words the grandfather rolled up his sleeves and was about to hit the old man in the mirror.

Suddenly the mirror slipped from his hand and fell to the floor with a loud crash. The grandfather, the boy, the two women, and the bridegroom all fell silent and stood staring dumbly at hundreds of pieces of broken glass beneath their feet.

The Bad Tiger

In a great forest there once lived a very bad tiger. Every night he would come out of his lair and steal into a radish patch kept by a poor old woman. There the bad tiger would trample all over the garden, eating the choicest and fattest radishes.

The poor woman came every morning to her radish patch and cried at the damage caused by the bad tiger. But she didn't know what to do, for the tiger was as strong as he was bad. She wondered and wondered how she could stop the tiger from eating her radishes every night. Finally, she hit upon a good plan.

One day, she met the tiger and said, "Mr. Tiger, why do you have to eat radishes all the time? Please come to my house, and I shall make some delicious, nourishing red bean gruel for you to eat."

The tiger was overjoyed at the prospect of a red bean gruel, for it was his favorite dish. "Thank you. I shall be over tonight," he said, licking his lips at the thought of the feast.

The old woman hurried home to prepare for the arrival of the bad tiger. First she lit a fire and heated up a large amount of charcoal. She put the glowing coals in a brazier and took the brazier outside to the back of her home.

Then, she floated some red-hot cayenne pepper on the water in her kitchen water jug.

Next, she stuck a large number of needles in the kitchen towel.

She then scattered cow dung all around the kitchen door, and spread a large straw mat, used in drying unhulled rice, out in the yard.

Finally, she brought out an A-frame, used on the back when carrying heavy loads and so-called because it is shaped like the letter "A" turned upside down. She propped the A-frame up against the back fence.

Now everything was ready. The old woman went back to her kitchen and pretended she was preparing the evening dinner.

Soon it was dark, and the bad tiger came sneaking to her house. The old woman heard the tiger outside and said, "Oh, it's you, Mr. Tiger. Please do come in." And she opened the front door, smiling her welcome at the bad tiger.

"My, it's cold tonight, isn't it, Mr. Tiger?" she said. "You won't mind, will you, bringing the charcoal brazier into the house from the back for me?"

"Of course," the bad tiger said, for he was in a good mood thinking of the feast he was about to have.

He went out back and was about to lift the brazier up when he noticed that the charcoal was almost out. "Say, old woman. The charcoal is almost out. There are hardly any red embers left."

The old woman answered from inside the house; "Is that so? Will you blow the embers for me? The charcoal will soon become red."

The bad tiger put his nose to the brazier and puffed and puffed. He blew so hard that some ashes whirled up and dropped into his eyes. The bad tiger hurriedly rubbed his eyes, but the more he rubbed the more they hurt. In pain, the bad tiger cried, "Old woman, old woman! I've got some ashes in my eyes. Help me!"

"Oh dear, I'm sorry," she said. "Try washing your eyes with water. You'll find some in the kitchen jug there."

The tiger did as he was told. But, as you will remember, the old woman had floated some red pepper on the water. The pepper got in both the tiger's eyes, and he was in greater pain than before. He thought he would surely go blind.

"Old woman, old woman!" he called, "my eyes are worse than before. What can I do?" Then, "Ooh! Ooh!" the bad tiger moaned, pressing his eyes with his front paws and stamping his feet in pain.

"Oh, is it that painful? Try wiping them with this kitchen towel."

The bad tiger was in great pain. He grabbed the towel she handed him and began rubbing his eyes frantically. But the needles in the towel pricked his eyes. Now the bad tiger became truly mad with pain.

Suddenly the bad tiger realized how he had been tricked by the old woman. Blindly he tried to run away. But, as soon as he stepped out the kitchen door, he slipped on the cow dung and fell head over heels on the ground.

30

The straw mat, which the old woman
had laid out in the back yard, saw all this and
came flying through the air. It quickly wrapped the
bad tiger in an incredible tight roll.

Next, the A-frame came trotting out from the back fence
and threw the tightly wrapped tiger on its back. Then, without a
word, the old woman put the frame on her back, went right down to the sea and threw the
bad tiger headlong into the waves.

That was the end of the bad tiger. Thereafter the old woman was able to raise her
radishes in peace. There was no longer a bad tiger to come and dig up her radish patch.

The Great Flood

Once upon a time, long, long ago, there lived a handsome boy named Talltree. He was called this because his father was a tree—a tree so tall that it almost reached the sky. His mother was a celestial being, a beautiful creature from Heaven who came down to earth from time to time. She often used to rest in the shade of the tall tree. In time she became the tree's wife and bore a healthy boy child, who became the Talltree of this story.

When Talltree was about eight years old, his mother left him beside his father, the great, tall tree, and returned to her home in the heavens.

One day a terrible storm arose suddenly. For days on end the rains poured down on earth, until all the ground was under water. Soon mountainous waves began sweeping toward the tall tree, the father of the young boy.

Father-tree became alarmed. He called to his child and said, "I shall soon be uprooted by this terrible storm. When I fall, you must climb into my branches and perch on my back. Otherwise, you will be drowned."

The storm became more and more violent. Lashed by screaming winds, great waves thundered against the trunk of the tree. Then came the fiercest gust of all, and the kingly tree fell with a crash.

Quickly the boy climbed on his father's back and held tightly to the branches. The great tree floated on the rushing waters. For days and days it drifted on and on, at the mercy of the angry waves.

One day they came upon a great number of ants struggling in the water. The poor ants, on the point of drowning, cried, "Save us! Save us!"

Talltree felt sorry for them and asked his father, "Shall we save the ants?"

"Yes," his father replied. "Climb up on my father's back," Talltree called to the ants, "and you will be saved. Hurry! Hurry!"

And Talltree helped the tired and weary ants get up out of the wind-whipped water onto the tree. The ants, of course, were very happy to be saved.

Soon, a great cloud of mosquitoes came flying through the storm. They, too, were weary, for nowhere was there any place to land and rest their tired wings.

"Help! Help!" the mosquitoes buzzed.

Again, Talltree asked, "Father, shall we save the mosquitoes?"

"Yes," his father replied.

So Talltree helped the tired mosquitoes alight on the leaves and branches of his father's back. The mosquitoes were also very grateful to be saved from the storm.

34

As Talltree and his father and the ants and the mosquitoes drifted along, they heard the cry of a child. In the waves they saw a boy about the same age as Talltree.

"Save me! Save me!" cried the boy.

Talltree felt sorry for the boy. "Let's save the boy too," he said.

But this time his father didn't answer.

Again the cries of the boy came pitifully across the raging waters. And again Talltree said, "Please, Father, let's save that boy."

Still there was no answer from Father-tree. Talltree pleaded with his father a third time, "Father, we must save that poor boy!"

The father finally answered: "Do as you wish. I leave it up to you."

Talltree was overjoyed and called to the boy to come and climb up onto his father's back. So the boy was saved too.

After a very long time, the father-tree, Talltree, the ants, the mosquitoes, and the boy who had been saved from the waves came to an island. It was the peak of the highest mountain in that country—a mountain as high as Paik Tu, the Mountain with a White Head, so-called because the snow never melted from its crest.

As soon as the tree reached the island, the ants and the mosquitoes thanked Talltree and took their departure.

The two boys were very hungry, for they had not eaten for many days. They wandered over the island searching for food and finally came upon a small straw-thatched hut.

"Please give us some food," the boys cried out. An old woman and two young girls came out. They welcomed the boys into the house and gave them food. One of the girls was the real daughter of the old woman and the other an adopted child.

The great flood and storm had destroyed everything on earth except this little island.

The only people left in the world were the two boys, the old woman, and the two girls. There was no other place where the boys could stay. So from that day on they lived with the old woman, working for her as servants.

It was a peaceful life. The days slipped into weeks, the weeks into months, and the months into years, and the boys grew into strong, fine youths.

As the old woman watched the boys grow into manhood, she thought to herself, "They will make fine husbands for my two girls."

One day, she told the two boys, "Whichever of you is the more skillful shall have my own daughter for his wife, and the other shall have my adopted girl."

Now the old woman's own daughter was very much the more beautiful of the two girls, and the boy who had been saved by Talltree during the flood wanted very much to marry her. He thought of a way to get her for his own wife.

"Grandma," he said, "Talltree has a strange power which none of the rest of us has. For example, you can mix a whole sack of millet in a pile of sand, and he can have the millet and the sand separated in no time. Let him try it and show you."

The old woman was surprised to hear this. "Is that so?" she said. "Come, Talltree, let me see if you really can do this amazing thing."

Talltree knew he was being tricked. He knew he certainly could do no such thing and he knew the other youth was planning to get him into trouble. So he refused. But the old woman was adamant. She was determined that Talltree should show her his strange and amazing power.

"If you don't do it, or if you can't do it, I won't let you marry my daughter," the old woman said.

Talltree saw he couldn't escape and sighed. "Very well, then," he said, "I'll try."

The old woman emptied a sack of millet into a pile of sand and thoroughly mixed them up together. Then she left, saying she would return in a short while to see how he was getting on.

Talltree gazed hopelessly at the pile of millet and sand. What was he to do? It was not humanly possible to sort the millet from the sand.

Suddenly, Talltree felt something bite his heel. He looked down, and there he saw a very large ant.

"What is troubling you, Talltree?" the ant asked. "I suppose you no longer remember me, but I am one of the ants you saved a long time ago in the flood. Let me help. Tell me, what's the matter?"

Talltree told the ant how he must separate the millet from the sand or else he would not be able to marry the old woman's daughter.

"Is that all the trouble? Then your worries are over. Just leave it to me."

No sooner had the ant said this than a great mass of ants came swarming from all over the place. They attacked the huge pile of sand and millet, each ant carrying a millet grain in its mouth and putting it into the sack placed nearby. Back and forth the ants hurried. In a twinkling of an eye all the millet was back in the sack.

When the old woman came back, she was amazed to find that Talltree had finished an impossible task in so short a time.

The other youth was surprised too, and annoyed that his trick had failed. But he still wished to marry the old woman's daughter and pleaded with her, "Please let me marry your real child."

The old woman hesitated. She thought for a moment and replied, "You are both very dear to me. I must be absolutely fair. Tonight will be a moonless night. I shall put my two daughters each in a separate room. One will be in the east room and the other in the west room. You two will stay outside and when I say 'ready,' you will both come into the house and go to the room of your choice. The girl you find there will be your bride. I'm sure this is the best and fairest plan."

That night the two youths waited outside for the old woman's command. Suddenly Talltree heard a mosquito flying close to his ear.

"Buzz, buzz," said the mosquito, in a wee voice. "Talltree, you must go to the east room. Buzz, buzz. Remember, it is the east room."

Talltree was overjoyed to hear this. He felt sure the mosquito was one he had saved during the flood.

"Ready!" the old woman cried out.

The two boys went into the house. While the other boy was still hesitating, Talltree went straight to the east room. There he found the good and beautiful daughter of the old woman. She became his wife.

The other youth could not complain. So he took the other girl for his wife.

Both couples were very happy. They had many, many children and lived happily ever after. In time, their children, and their grandchildren, and their great-grandchildren spread throughout the world. And again the earth was filled with people.

The Pumpkin Seeds

There once lived in the same village two brothers. The elder was greedy and miserly. The younger was a gentle and open-hearted man. The older brother lived in a great mansion and had everything he wanted. Yet he was always complaining, as if by habit, that he led a hard life. On the other hand, his younger brother was poor and lived a humble life. But he never once complained.

One spring, swallows from some faraway southern country came and made a nest under the eaves of the poor brother's house. By the time the early summer breeze was rippling the green rice seedlings, the swallow had hatched its eggs, and the nest was full

of young birds. From morning to night, the baby birds made merry music under the eaves of the poor man's straw-thatched house. The kind-hearted younger brother placed a wide board under the nest to catch the baby birds, in case they fell from the nest to the ground below. The parent swallows busily carried food to their young and worked hard to make them grow big. And they did grow big, with each passing day.

One day, while the parent birds were away looking for food, a large green snake slid down the roof of the hut. As it approached the swallow's nest, it raised its head and peered inside, as if to say, "Yum, yum! These young birds will make a tasty meal." The snake poised itself to strike, showing its fangs. Of course, the baby swallows had never seen such a horrible sight before. They flapped their small wings in fear and tried with all their might to fly away. But their wings were too weak. One little bird succeeded in taking off only to crash to the ground.

The young brother heard the commotion and came running out of the house. He saw the snake just in time and, with a great cry, chased it away.

The bird that had fallen from the nest had broken a leg. "Oh, you poor little thing," the brother said, "it must be painful." He gently lifted the bird from the ground, put medicine on its leg, and wound it carefully with a bit of white cloth.

Ten, twenty days passed. The baby swallow with the broken leg was soon well again. It was strong enough to fly now. It no longer needed to wait for its mother to bring it food. It swooped through the great sky, swiftly and freely, in search of insects and bugs.

Summer passed and autumn came. The swallows left for their winter home in the south. The swallow with the broken leg was now a big bird. Reluctantly, it too joined the migrating birds and left the village.

Early the next spring, the swallows came back to their old nest. They had travelled a long way, over seas and over mountains, but they had not forgotten their old home. The

happy swallows swooped under the eaves of the straw-thatched hut. The humble hut of the younger brother again echoed to the merry chirping of birds.

The swallow that had broken its leg the year before also returned. As if to repay the young brother's kindness, it carried in its beak a pumpkin seed. The bird dropped the seed in a corner of the poor brother's yard, where it soon sprouted and shot forth a tendril that gradually climbed up to the roof of the poor man's home.

By autumn, three big pumpkins, so large that each made an armful, were ripening on the vine. The younger brother was overjoyed and cut down one pumpkin. "This is a rare thing to have such large pumpkins. One such pumpkin alone would be enough to feed many people. I must take some of it to the villagers." So thinking, the younger brother cut the pumpkin in two.

What should happen then! Out of the pumpkin trooped a host of carpenters. Some carried axes, some saws, some planes, and some hammers. Each carried some kind of tool. After the carpenters had all come out, there came a flow of building materials—timbers, planks, window frames, and doors. In a twinkling of an eye, the carpenters built a large mansion and then disappeared from sight.

The younger brother was completely dumbfounded at this strange and unexpected happening. He then began wondering what the other pumpkins might contain. He gingerly cut open the second pumpkin.

Out came a host of servants. There were farmhands too, with plows and spades and rakes. There were also maids, carrying water jugs on their heads, and seamstresses, with needles in their hands. When they had all come out, they lined up before the younger brother and, bowing deeply, said together, "Master, we are here to serve you. Please tell us what you would like us to do."

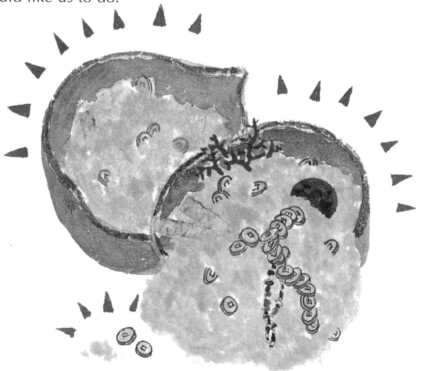

From the third pumpkin there flowed silver and gold in such quantities that the younger brother was completely dazed. Overnight, he became the richest man in the village, and soon he was the owner of vast lands, purchased with the money that had come from the third pumpkin.

The greedy older brother was totally green with envy. His every waking thought was how to become as wealthy as his younger brother. One day he came over to visit his brother, whom he had ignored for so long in the past. Slyly he asked, "Say, my dear brother, how did you manage to become so rich?"

The honest younger brother did not hide anything, but told him everything that had happened. The older brother, when he heard the story, thought greedily of a plan. As soon as early summer came the next year, he took a baby swallow from one of the nests in the eaves of his house and broke its leg. Then he put medicine on the broken leg, bound it with a piece of white cloth, and put the bird back into its nest. In autumn this swallow flew away to the south.

The older brother could scarcely contain his joy. "I've only to wait a short while longer. Then that swallow will return and bring me a pumpkin seed too."

Sure enough, the swallow whose leg had been broken on purpose returned the next spring to the elder brother's house and brought back a pumpkin seed in its mouth.

The older brother took the seed and planted it in a corner of his yard. Every day he gave it water and cried, "Hurry and grow big! Hurry and grow big!" He did not forget to mix a lot of manure into the ground where the pumpkin seed had been planted.

In time, out came a green sprout. It grew and grew, stretching its vine up over the roof. In time, too, three pumpkins took shape and ripened. The pumpkins were much larger than those that had grown at his younger brother's house.

"How lucky I am!" the older brother said. "Thank Heaven! Now everything is set. I shall be much richer than my younger brother." He could not help dancing about in joy and anticipation.

Finally the time came and he cut the first pumpkin. But what should appear? Not carpenters, but a swarm of demons with cudgels in their hands.

"You inhuman and greedy monster! Now you'll get what you deserve!" the demons cried, and they began beating the older brother in turns.

After a while the demons disappeared. The older brother was all blue with bruises, but still he had not learned his lesson. "This time, for sure, I'll find much treasure," he thought, and cut open the second pumpkin.

But this time a host of money collectors came out crying, "Pay your debts! Pay your debts! If you don't we'll take away everything we can lay our hands on."

And they did! They grabbed everything in sight. In a flash, the older brother's home was completely emptied of all it contained, leaving only a shell.

The older brother cursed himself for having cut open the second pumpkin, but it was too late. And still he could not give up his dreams of an easy fortune. He stuck a knife into the third pumpkin and split it open. What should come out but a flood of yellow muddy water. It came bubbling out in an unending stream. It flowed in such quantities that soon his home, his garden, and his fields were covered with yellow mud.

The older brother finally could stand it no longer. With a cry of anguish he fled to the shelter of his younger brother's house.

The kind-hearted younger brother greeted him with open arms and treated him very well. The older brother suddenly realized how selfish and mean he had been. He became a humble and contrite man.

The younger brother gave his elder brother half of everything he had—paddies, fields, servants, and money—and from that time on the two lived on the most friendly of terms.

The Tiger and the Rabbit

Once a hungry old tiger was walking through the woods, looking for something to eat. By chance he came upon a baby rabbit. The old tiger's eyes glistened to see such a juicy morsel.

"I'm going to eat you up," he told the rabbit.

The baby rabbit, though very small, was a clever fellow. He coolly answered, "Just wait, Mr Tiger. I'm still too young and small to make a good meal. I have something much tastier for you. I shall give you some rice cakes. When you toast them over a fire, they are really delicious."

48

As he said this, the rabbit stealthily picked up eleven small white stones. He showed them to the tiger.

The greedy tiger became very interested. "But," he said, "how do you eat these?"

The rabbit answered, "Here, I'll show you. You toast them over a fire until they are red-hot, and then you eat them in one gulp. I'll go and find some firewood so that you can have some right away." The rabbit gathered together some twigs and sticks and started a fire. The tiger put the eleven stones on the fire and watched them toast.

When the stones were getting hot and red, the rabbit said, "Mr. Tiger, wait a while. If you put soy sauce on the cakes, they will taste even more delicious. I shall get some for you. You must wait now and don't eat any while I am gone.... Let's see, there are ten rice cakes, aren't there?" So saying, the baby rabbit skipped into the woods and ran away.

As the stones reddened with the heat, the tiger began licking his lips in anticipation. He started counting what he thought were rice cakes.

"One, two, three.... Why," he said in surprise, "there are eleven cakes, not ten."

He started counting them over again, but, no matter how many times he counted, there was always one too many.

"The baby rabbit said there were ten. If I ate one, he wouldn't know the difference," the tiger said to himself.

So he quickly took the reddest one from the fire, popped it in his mouth, and gulped it down greedily. But, oh, it was hot! So very, very hot! The tiger not only burnt his mouth and tongue, but his stomach as well. He squirmed with pain. He moaned and groaned and rolled all over the ground.

All of which served the old tiger right for being so greedy. It was some time before he could eat anything again.

One day, much later, the tiger met the baby rabbit again.

"Say you, you bad rabbit! What a time you gave me the other day. I'll not let you go this time. Now I'll really eat you up." And the tiger's eyes burned with anger.

But the baby rabbit did not look a bit frightened. With a smile, he answered, "Don't be so angry, Mr. Tiger. Please listen to me. I have found a way to catch hundreds and thousands of sparrows. All you have to do is to keep perfectly still with your mouth wide open. The sparrows will come flying right into your mouth and make a nice feast for you."

The old tiger licked his lips and asked, "Oh, is that so? What else am I supposed to do?"

"Oh, it isn't difficult at all. All you need to do is to look up at the sky and keep your mouth open. I'll chase the sparrows out of the bamboo thicket into your mouth."

Once again the old tiger did as he was told.

The baby rabbit hopped into the bamboo thicket and set fire to a pile of dry leaves and twigs. The sound made by the burning leaves and twigs was just like the fluttering of thousands of sparrows.

The tiger, meanwhile, kept gazing up at the sky, his mouth wide open. "Why, it does sound as if the birds are flying this way," he thought. And he kept right on staring up at the sky, his mouth wide open, waiting for the sparrows to fly into it.

From a distance, the baby rabbit cried, "Shoo! Shoo! Shoo!" pretending he was chasing a multitude of sparrows.

"Mr. Tiger, Mr. Tiger, a lot of birds are flying your way now. Don't move! Just wait a while longer." So saying, the baby rabbit scampered away to safety.

The fire came closer and closer to the tiger, and the noise became louder and louder. The tiger was sure the birds were coming his way, and he patiently waited. Soon the noise was all about him, but not a single sparrow popped into his mouth.

"That's funny," thought the tiger, and he took his eyes from the sky and looked around him. To his surprise, there was one great ocean of fire all about him as far as he could see.

The tiger became frantic with fear as he fought his way through the burning woods. Finally he managed to come through alive, but his fur was all sizzled black. And his skin looked like newly tanned hide.

It was soon winter. Once again the tiger became ravenously hungry. As he stalked through the forest looking for food, he came to the bank of a river. There he saw his old friend, the baby rabbit, eating some vegetables.

The tiger roared angrily at the rabbit, "How dare you fool me about the sparrows! I won't let you get away with anything this time. I will eat you up for sure." He ground his teeth and ran up to the rabbit.

The rabbit smiled as usual and said, "Hello, Mr. Tiger, it's quite some time since we last met, isn't it? Look, I was just fishing with my tail in the river. I caught a big one, and it was delicious. Don't you think river fish are very tasty?"

The hungry tiger gulped with hunger and said, "You were fishing with your tail? Show me how it is done."

"It isn't very easy," the rabbit replied, "but I'm sure you will be able to do it. All you need to do is to put your tail in the water and shut your eyes. I shall go up the river a little and chase the fish this way. Remember, you mustn't move. Just wait a little, and you'll have many fish biting at your tail." The old tiger did exactly what the rabbit told him. He put his tail into the river, closed his eyes, and waited.

The rabbit ran up the river bank and hopped about here and there, pretending to chase the fish down to where the tiger was waiting. The winter day was beginning to end, and the water became colder and colder.

"The fish are beginning to swim your way, Mr. Tiger," the rabbit shouted. "They will be biting on your tail any minute. Don't move!" Then the rabbit ran away.

The river began to freeze over slowly. The old tiger moved his tail a wee bit. It was heavy. "Ah, good! I must have caught a lot of fish on my tail. Just a while longer and I shall have a good catch," he told himself.

He waited quietly and motionless until midnight. "Now I shall have lots of succulent fish to eat," he thought.

So he tried to pull his tail out. But it wouldn't move! What had happened? Why, his tail was frozen tightly in the ice.

"Oh, I have been tricked again by that rabbit," moaned the tiger. But, it was too late to do anything.

When it became light, the villagers came to the river and found the old tiger trapped in the ice. Thus the greedy old tiger was finally caught and taken away. And that was one tiger who never ate another rabbit.

The Green Leaf

D ay in and day out, the rain poured down in sheets. The small river flowing by the village rose higher and higher. One day the dikes broke. The muddy river water surged through the gap, sweeping everything in its path—houses, people, cows, and horses. Everywhere there was death and devastation.

Just then there appeared in the raging waters an old man, rowing a small boat. He was a gentle and kind man. He could not bear to remain in safety while listening to the cries of people stranded on treetops and on rooftops. He rowed his small boat here and there, helping as many people as he could to places of safety.

Just as he was about to leave he saw a small child struggling in the water. He pulled the child into his boat. He next saw a deer swimming by. The deer too he saved. A little while later a snake came swimming by. The old man looked carefully and saw that it had hurt itself. It couldn't swim very well. A snake is not a very pleasant thing, but the old man felt sorry for it.

He reached into the swirling waters and pulled the snake into the boat. When he reached high ground, the old man let the snake and the deer go free. But the child had nowhere to go. He had lost his home, his parents, and his brothers and sisters. He was now an orphan. The old man felt sorry for the poor little boy. He seemed such a clever fellow, with fine features. Since the old man was childless, he decided to adopt the boy as his own. "You will become my boy from this day," the old man said, and from then on he cared for him as if he were his own child.

One day much later the old man was puttering about the house. Suddenly the same deer that he had saved during the flood came to the house. The deer came right up to the old man inside the house, nudged him with its nose as though glad to see him, and made happy sounds in its throat. Then the deer took hold of the old man's sleeve in its mouth and started pulling and kept pulling as though wanting the old man to follow it.

"You want me to go outside with you, do you?" the old man said. "Yes, that must be it." So the old man went outside with the deer. The deer kept going on ahead, and the old man followed. On and on, toward the mountains. Up and up they climbed. The old man didn't know where they were going. Neither could he imagine what the deer wanted.

Just as they crossed a mountain divide, the deer stopped short and waited for the old man to catch up. There in the mountain was a cave. The deer led the old man to the mouth of the cave and then went in ahead. The old man followed. And in the middle of the cave he found a large box filled to overflowing with gold and silver, shining with such dazzling brightness as to blind the eyes. The old man took this treasure home.

Thanks to the deer, the old man was now very wealthy. He bought a large mansion and many fields and paddies. He came to live a life of plenty. And his adopted son quickly learned to live an easy-going life. He learned to be selfish and extravagant.

He spent money like water, he made friends with good-for-nothing youths, and he frittered his days away in idleness.

The old man began to worry over the future of his son. He tried to advise the young man, but his words fell on deaf ears. Eventually the young man came to talk back to his foster father. He went from bad to worse and, in time, even started spreading a very bad lie about his father.

"That old man didn't get his money from the deer. That's a big lie. He stole all of it during the flood from people who were washed away." This was the lie the young man spread all over the village. When this lie came to the ears of the overlord, the old man was hauled off to the overlord's castle for questioning.

"That's simply not true," the old man insisted. "The deer really did lead me to the money in a cave."

But no matter how earnestly and how often the old man repeated this to the castle officials, they still doubted him.

"Even your adopted son, whom you brought up yourself for so many years, says you stole your wealth," they said. "Isn't that sufficient proof of your crime?" And they threw him into the castle dungeon.

There was nothing the old man could do about it. He spent long hours and days in the dungeon, crying and waiting for the day he would be brought out to hear his sentence.

But one day while the old man sat despondently in the dungeon, something came moving across the floor. It was the snake the old man had saved during the flood.

The snake quietly slithered across the cell to where the old man was sitting and suddenly bit him sharply on the ankle. Then it quickly slipped out again.

The old man was very upset. "How unfortunate I am! No matter how lowly a creature may be, to think that it would do such a terrible thing after I went to the trouble of saving its life! I should never have shown pity for that snake." First it was his adopted son and now it was the snake. The old man had saved both from the raging waters, and they had turned against him in ingratitude. The thought filled the old man with such anguish that he felt his heart would burst. He pressed the snake bite with his hands and let the tears stream unashamedly down his cheeks.

Suddenly the snake once again came into his cell. This time it was carrying something in its mouth. It was a green leaf. The snake applied the green leaf to the spot where it had bitten the old man and then quickly disappeared again.

Then a strange thing happened. No sooner had the green leaf been placed on the wound than the pain disappeared, and the swelling also went down.

58

"What was the snake trying to do?" pondered the old man. "First it comes and bites me and then it brings a green leaf that heals me. Why?"

But before he could think further, there was a great commotion outside his cell. "It's terrible, terrible!" the jailers were shouting. "What shall we do? The lord's wife has just been bitten by a snake. There's no time to call a doctor."

The old man suddenly realized the meaning of the snake's behavior. He shouted, "Let me cure her! I have a wonderful medicine for snake bites!"

The jailers looked doubtfully at the old man. But it was no time to stop and argue. They let the old man out of his cell and rushed him off to where the overlord's wife lay moaning and suffering in pain. All the old man did was to press the green leaf lightly against the snake bite, and the great lady was completely healed.

The overlord was very pleased and had the old man brought before him. "Old man, where did you get that wonderful medicine?" the lord asked.

The old man then told the overlord all that had happened to him from the time he saved his adopted son, the deer, and the snake in the great flood, until the time the snake appeared in his cell.

"Even such a lowly creature as the snake knows how to repay a debt of gratitude. But what kind of man would betray the foster father who saved his life?" the lord said in great anger. Then the lord ordered his men to bring the boy to the castle and to throw him into the dungeon.

The kind old man was praised highly and given many gifts. As a last request, he asked that his ungrateful son be released from prison. The overlord was deeply impressed by the compassion of the old man and immediately granted his request. Then the old man and his son made their way home together. The youth had learned his lesson. Not only once, but twice, had his life been saved by his foster father. From then on, he became a changed person and grew into a good man.

The Three Little Girls

Deep in the mountains there stood a lonely hut. In this hut lived a mother and her three small daughters. The eldest girl was named Haisuni, the second Talsuni, and the youngest Peolsuni.

One day the mother had to leave home to take some firewood to the market to sell. Before she left she called her three daughters and said, "Listen, Haisuni, Talsuni, and Peolsuni. Do be careful while I am gone, for there is a very bad tiger roaming the woods nearby. Don't ever open the door to anybody until I get back. Otherwise you might be eaten up by the bad tiger."

So saying, the mother stepped out the door and went on her way.

Just as she was leaving, the bad tiger happened to pass the house. He was very hungry and was in search of food. He saw the mother leave the house and thought, "Ho ho! Now's my chance! Now that the mother's gone, I'll be able to eat those three young girls of hers. They should make a tasty dinner for me. How nice that would be!"

The tiger waited a while to make sure that the mother would not return. Then, when he thought the time was ripe, he crept up to the house and called out in his sweetest voice, "Haisuni, Talsuni, Peolsuni—Mother has just come back. Please open the door."

Of course, no matter how sweetly the tiger spoke, his voice was not the voice of their mother. So the eldest girl, Haisuni, asked, "Is that really you, Mother? It doesn't sound a bit like you."

"Why, of course I'm your mother," the tiger answered. "I was invited to a feast and there I sang so many songs that my voice has become hoarse."

The second daughter, Talsuni, then asked, "If you are really our mother, then show us your eyes. We would be able to tell for sure."

Hearing this, the tiger put his blood-shot eyes to a knothole in the front door and peered into the house.

Talsuni saw the red eyes and drew back in surprise. "Oh my! Why are your eyes so red?"

The tiger, a bit confused, hurriedly explained, "I dropped in at Grandfather's house and helped grind some red pepper pods. Some of the pepper got into my eyes, and that's why they are so red."

The third daughter, Peolsuni, next asked, "If that's true, then let us see your hands. We could really tell then whether you are our mother or not."

The tiger put his hairy, yellow paws to a crack in the door.

Peolsuni peeked through the crack and cried, "Why! your hands are all yellow!"

"Yes, my child," the tiger said, "I was helping our relatives in the next village plaster their house with yellow mud. That's why my hands are so yellow."

In this way the very clever tiger fooled all the girls completely. Sure that it was their mother, they unlocked the front door. And who should come in but a huge, yellow tiger!

"My, you children looked after the house well, didn't you?" the tiger said. "As a reward, Mother will cook a nice dinner for you." The tiger went into the kitchen, his eyes shining with greed.

The three girls stood huddled in a corner, quivering with fear. "What shall we do? What shall we do? We shall soon be eaten up by the tiger."

The three girls quickly ran out of the house. Then tiptoeing softly away, they quickly climbed up a pine tree growing near the well. There they hid quietly in the branches.

The tiger soon noticed that the girls were no longer in the house. "Haisuni, Talsuni, Peolsuni," he called, "where are you?"

And the bad tiger looked here and there, inside and outside the house, everywhere, but nowhere were the girls to be seen. The tiger passed the well and happened to glance in. There he saw in the water the reflection of the three girls hiding in the branches of the pine tree.

"My, children!" the tiger said. "What are you doing up there? I want to come up too, but it looks difficult. Tell Mother how to climb the tree."

At this, Haisuni called down, "There's some sesame oil in the kitchen cupboard. Rub some of the oil on the trunk of the tree. Then you can easily climb up."

Quickly the tiger went into the house, got the oil, and rubbed it on the trunk of the tree. Then he tried to climb, but the oil made him slip all the more, and try as he might, he could not reach the girls.

Once again, the tiger looked up into the tree and said, "Be good children, dears, and tell me truly how to climb the tree."

Talsuni, the second daughter, unthinkingly let her tongue slip and said, "There's an ax in the shed. If you cut some notches in the tree trunk, then you can climb up."

Quickly, the tiger went for the ax and began cutting footholds with it. One step at a time, he climbed up and up toward the girls.

The three sisters were desperate. They were sure they would be eaten up. They raised their eyes toward the sky and prayed to the God of Heaven. "Please help us, God. Please send down your golden well bucket," they prayed.

Their prayers were answered, and from the top of a cloud down came a golden well bucket. The three sisters climbed into the bucket and were snatched up, out of the teeth of danger, into the clouds.

When the tiger saw this, he too prayed to the God of Heaven, "Please send down a well bucket for me also."

Once again, a well bucket came down from the clouds. But this time the rope of the bucket was old and rotten. The tiger, nevertheless, climbed trustingly into the bucket, and it started rising. But when he was halfway up to the clouds, the rope suddenly broke, and the tiger came crashing to earth, right in the middle of a millet field.

That is why the root tops of millet are mottled to this day. The reddish spots are from the blood of the tiger which splattered all over the millet field.

On the other hand, the three sisters who climbed to Heaven were each given a special task. Haisuni was made to shine in the sky during the day. Talsuni was made to shine at

night. And Peolsuni was to twinkle on nights when Talsuni slept or was on her way from the sky to rest. That is why the sun is called Haisuni, the moon Talsuni, and the stars Peolsuni. To this very day, the three sisters keep at their tasks, taking their turns at brightening the whole world with their light.

The Snake and the Toad

Once there lived a very kind and gentle girl in a remote country village. She was very poor and barely managed to make a living for herself and her old mother, whom she had to care for all alone.

One day the girl was in the kitchen, just scooping up freshly cooked rice and putting it into a large bowl to carry to the dinner table. Suddenly a toad appeared in the kitchen as if from nowhere. It crawled over the floor laboriously, dragging its body, right up to where the girl was standing. Then it jumped heavily up onto the kitchen hearth. On the hearth were a few grains of rice which the girl had spilled while emptying the pot. The toad ate up the rice hungrily.

"My, you must really be hungry," the kind girl said. "Here, I'll give you some more."

And she spilled about half a ladleful of rice out on the hearth. The toad looked up at the girl in gratitude and then quickly gobbled up that rice too, all the while wriggling his puffy throat.

From that day on the girl and the toad became fast friends. The toad did not go anywhere. He made his home in a corner of the kitchen and would come out at mealtimes to eat his share of rice right out of the girl's hands. This way of life continued day after day, until one whole year had passed. By this time the toad had grown into a huge creature.

Now, this village had been troubled for a long, long time by a huge snake that lived in a nest on the outskirts of the hamlet. It was a very bad snake. It played havoc with the rice paddies and the vegetable fields. It stole cows and horses. It even kidnapped women and children and dragged them away to its nest, where it ate them up at leisure. Not once or twice this had happened, but many, many times.

The villagers knew the hide-out of the snake. Its nest was in a huge cave in a rocky

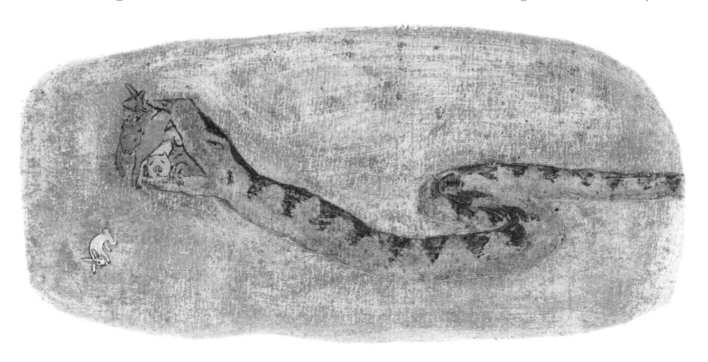

hill just outside the village. Master bowmen and famed marksmen came in turn to the great snake's nest to try and kill the monster, but none succeeded. Year after year the snake continued to harass the villagers. The people lived constantly in fear and under the threat of death. They never knew when the snake would come out from its nest and pounce upon the unsuspecting. They never knew where it would strike next.

The toad's friend, the kind-hearted girl, soon came to the point where she could not bear to see all the suffering. Without really knowing when, she found herself thinking, "The villagers must be saved. There must be some way. Isn't there a good scheme?"

But when bows and arrows and guns had failed to kill the snake, what could one single, weak girl do? After much pondering, the girl finally decided that she would give up her own life to save the villagers from this curse.

"That's it!" she thought. "If a large number of people can be saved, it doesn't matter what happens to me. I shall offer myself to be eaten by the great snake, and I shall beg the snake never again to terrorize our village. Where guns and arrows have failed, my sincere pleas might succeed."

Her old mother was now dead, and she was all alone in the world except for her friend the toad. So, once she had made her mind up, she put on her little shoes with their turned-up toes and slipped out of the house. Just before leaving she called the toad and, wiping the tears from her eyes, said, "We have lived happily together for a long time, haven't we? But today is our last day. I must say goodbye. There will be no one to give you your rice tomorrow. When you become hungry, you will have to go out and find your own food."

The toad, of course, had no way of understanding the language of human beings. But the girl spoke to it in simple and gentle words, just as if she were talking to a child. All the while the toad squatted on the hearth gazing steadily up at the girl's face.

The girl finally made her way to the snake's nest in the rocky hill outside the village. Forgetting her fear and her sorrow in her desire to save all the villagers, she stepped right

up to the mouth of the huge snake's large nest. "I have come in place of the villagers to offer you my life," she said.

"Please eat me. But, after this, please never again bother the village people."

Nothing happened, so the girl continued speaking in this way for a long time. Soon night drew near, and darkness began to fall over the countryside.

Finally, when the last light of day faded, the earth began to tremble, and the snake came out of its hole. Its many scales were a gleaming green, its red tongue was like a fiery flame. When the girl saw the terrible appearance of the snake, she fainted on the spot and fell to the ground.

Just then a single streak of white poison flashed toward the snake. It came from the toad which the girl had cared for with such kindness. No one knew when it had come, but there it was, squatting right beside the girl. And though it was small compared to the snake, it was squirting poison with all its might to protect the unconscious girl.

But the snake was not to be beaten so easily. It began spewing poison right back at the toad. Thus the snake and the toad matched poison against poison, the jets of poison crossing and criss-crossing in the air like two sharp darts. Neither would give in. This continued for one hour, two hours. There was no sound of clashing swords, no shouts of battle. For all that, it was a deadly fight, waged in grim silence.

Gradually, the snake's poison began to weaken. On the other hand, the toad's poison became stronger and stronger. And yet, the fight still continued.

Suddenly the snake let out a great gasp and fell down on the rocky hillside. Its great body twitched once, twice, and then it was dead. At the same time the toad, worn out with its struggle, fell dead too. The battle was finally over.

A lone villager happened to pass by the scene of the fighting the next morning and found the small girl still unconscious. He took her to her home and nursed her back to health. In this way, not only was the girl saved but the whole village as well, thanks to the heroic struggle of a lone toad whom the girl had befriended. Now that the evil snake was dead, the villagers were able to live in peace and quiet.

The Grateful Tiger

Once upon a time a huge tiger lay groaning and moaning by the roadside. A young student happened to pass by and see the suffering animal. He drew near, half in fear, and asked, "What is the matter, tiger? Have you hurt yourself?"

The tiger, tears filling his eyes, opened its mouth as if to show the student that there was something wrong inside.

"Let me see," the student said, "maybe I can help." The student peered into the tiger's mouth and saw a sharp bone splinter stuck in the animal's throat.

"Oh, you poor thing!" the student said. "There's a bone stuck in your throat. Here, let me take it out. Easy now, it will soon be better." The student stuck his hand into the tiger's mouth and gently pulled the bone out.

The tiger licked the student's hands and looked up into his face with tears of relief and gratitude, as if to say, "Thank you, thank you for your kindness." Then, bowing low again and again, the tiger walked toward the woods, turning to look back from time to time at the student.

That night, as he slept, the student had a strange dream. A beautiful girl, whom he had never seen before, appeared in his sleep and said, "I am the tiger you saved today. Thanks to your gentle kindness, I was spared much pain and suffering. I shall surely show my gratitude to you some day." With that, the beautiful girl faded away.

Many years passed. The young student who had helped the tiger was now ready to take his final examinations in the capital city. As he rode along toward the capital he was thinking that if he passed these examinations he would become a government official and would one day become rich and famous. But many, many students came to take the test from all over the country. In fact, there were so many applicants that it was very difficult to pass the examinations.

The student prayed in his heart that he would be one of the fortunate ones to pass the difficult examinations. But it was not to be so. He failed. There were just too many people ahead of him. He was very downhearted. "I have come such a long, long way to the city. But I suppose it can't be helped. I'll return home, study hard, and try again next year." In this way he resigned himself to his failure and prepared to return to his home in the country the next day.

That night, however, the young student again had a dream. Again the strange beautiful girl appeared and said, "Don't be discouraged. It's still too early to despair. I shall repay you for the kindness you showed me many years ago. Tomorrow a wild tiger will run loose through the city. That tiger will be me. However, no gunman or bowman will be able to kill me. I am sure the king will offer a big reward to anybody who succeeds in getting rid of me. At that time, offer your services. Just take one shot at me. You will be sure to hit me."

The student was astounded to hear this and quickly replied, "No, no! I can't possibly do such a thing. Just because of one little kindness, I cannot take your life."

"No, you mustn't think that way," the tiger said, still in the form of a young woman. "I am very old and just about ready to die. I have very few days left to live. Since that's so, it's my wish to show you my tremendous gratitude. Don't say another word—just do as I have told you."

The student would not listen to the tiger. "But how can I do such a thing? I cannot commit such a cowardly act just to win fame for myself."

Suddenly the girl flared in anger. "Why can't you understand?" she said. "By saying such things you are rejecting my sincere feelings of gratitude. Stop talking and do just as I have told you. Oh, one more thing—a number of people will be hurt. Go then to the Temple of Hungryung and ask for some bean paste. If you apply this bean paste to the wounds of the people, they will soon be healed." The girl repeated her instructions many times and then faded away from his dreams. It was then that the young student woke up.

The student pondered over the strange dream that he had had and waited in restless anticipation for the day to break. And, sure enough, as dawn broke a wild tiger appeared in the city and ran wild through the streets.

The capital was in an uproar. Bowmen and gunmen were dispatched to kill the tiger. But no matter how carefully they aimed their weapons, they could not hit the animal. The people were now in a terrible panic. Many had been hurt. Finally the king sent out a messenger to announce a royal proclamation. "Hear ye! Hear ye!" the messenger cried. "The King proclaims that anyone who shoots the tiger shall be greatly rewarded. A high court

rank shall be
bestowed upon him and
a great treasure of rice shall be his."

The student was surprised to hear this. A high court rank, and a treasure of rice. The rice alone would be enough to maintain a large retinue of retainers. And then he remembered the dream of the night before.

So the young student went before the king and said, "O King! I shall kill the tiger." The king gladly gave his consent for the student to hunt the rampaging animal.

The student went to the main street of the capital where the tiger was prowling about. Without even taking aim, the student took one shot at the animal. The wild tiger, that had the whole city in confusion, dropped dead.

That very day the student was made a nobleman and given his reward of a treasure of rice. Nor did the student forget about the bean paste from the Temple of Hungryung. He got the paste and applied it to the wounds of the people who had been hurt. Their injuries healed so quickly that his fame spread throughout the country.

Now, the story doesn't say so, but it is easy to imagine that the famous nobleman found for his wife the same beautiful girl whose shape the tiger had used in the young student's dreams—and that they lived together happily for many, many long years.

The Three Princesses

Once there was a king who had three daughters. All three of the princesses were gentle, noble, and beautiful. But of the three the youngest was regarded by all as the loveliest girl in the land.

One moonlit night the three princesses climbed a small hill behind their father's castle to view the beautiful moon. Suddenly, a huge eagle swept down as if from nowhere and, in a flash, snatched the three princesses up in its giant talons. Then it rose into the air and disappeared with the princesses.

The whole castle was thrown into turmoil. The king's bowmen and gunmen came rushing up the hill. But it was too late. The eagle was nowhere to be seen. All they could do was to gaze into the sky and bemoan the fate of the three girls.

The king's sorrow at losing all three of his daughters at one stroke was pitiful to behold. He immediately sent out his soldiers to proclaim throughout the land that anyone who succeeded in saving the three princesses would be given half his kingdom. In addition, he promised to give the savior of the girls his youngest and most beautiful daughter in marriage.

But who was there to save the princesses?

There was one, and only one, man in the whole country who knew where the princesses had been taken. He was a young warrior living deep in the mountains. This young man had left all human habitation behind and gone far into the mountain wilderness to improve his martial skills. At night this solitary warrior used to mount his horse and practice with his spear and sword.

One night, as usual, the warrior had put on his armour and helmet and was spurring his horse in mock combat when he saw a huge eagle flying toward him. When it came near he saw, clutched in its talons, three young girls. By the light of the full moon, the warrior followed the flight of the great bird, and spurred his horse over hills and valleys in pursuit. All night long he chased the giant bird and, near dawn, he saw the eagle alight at the base of a huge cliff and disappear from sight.

The warrior whipped his horse on, and after a time reached the spot at the bottom of the high cliff where the eagle had disappeared. Here he spotted a hole in the base of the cliff. This, the warrior thought, must be the entrance to the Land-below-the-earth, a place he had heard about only in rumors. After carefully studying the entrance, the warrior was certain that he was right.

The warrior had also heard that in the Land-below-the-earth there lived a terrible ogre who slept, once he fell asleep, for three months and ten days. This ogre had many henchmen and kept a large number of eagles, which he used to steal lots of treasures and kidnap people from the earth above. Before he returned to his lonely home, the warrior marked with great care the entrance to the Land-below-the-earth.

By next morning the story of the disappearance of the three princesses and the king's proclamation had reached even this remote part of the mountains where the warrior was

in training. The young man set off immediately for the king's palace and was allowed to see the king.

"O King," the young man said, "I shall bring back the three princesses."

The king answered, "Please do whatever you can."

The young warrior then asked the king for the loan of the five strongest men among the king's soldiers. Then he began preparations for his venture into the Land-below-the-earth. He prepared a strong rope 300 miles in length, a basket large enough to hold one person, and a silver bell. Then the young warrior set off for the mountains, accompanied by the five soldiers.

After many days, he came once again to the entrance of the Land-below-the-earth. He tied the basket to one end of the rope and at the other end the silver bell. His idea was to lower the basket by the rope, and when the bell was rung, to pull it up.

The warrior ordered one of the soldiers to go down in the basket first. The man had gone down only 3 miles when the bell rang "Tinkle, tinkle." The man was hauled up to the surface. He was white with terror.

A second soldier went down as far as 15 miles, but he too became afraid and was pulled back. A third, and then a fourth, was sent down, but each was overcome with fear part way down and had to be hauled out. Even the strongest of the soldiers, the fifth man, could only go down 150 miles.

Finally the young warrior himself entered the basket and was lowered into the hole. Down, down he went. There seemed no end. Just as the 300-mile-long rope ran out, the warrior touched bottom. He had reached the Land-below-the-earth!

There he found thousands of large and small houses lined up, row after row. Among them he noticed one that was larger than the rest. It stood without any roof. "This," he thought, "must be the home of the ogre." The young warrior racked his brains for some scheme by which he could enter the house of the ogre, who was chief of the Land-below-the-earth.

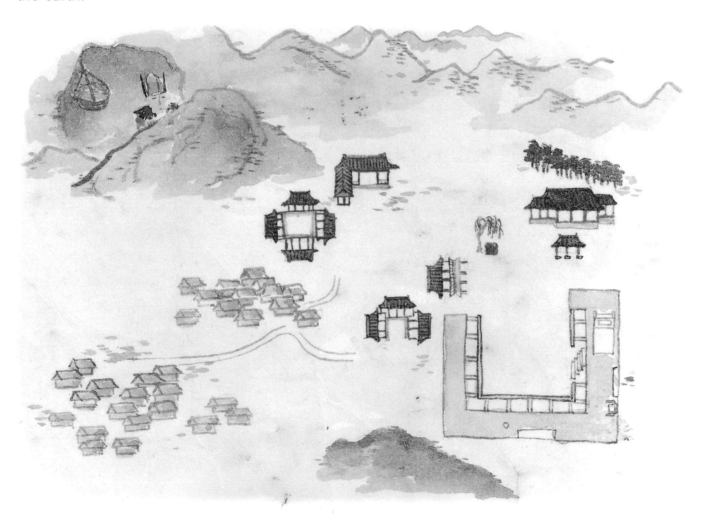

As he approached the house, he noticed a well in the yard, and beside the well there stood a large willow tree. The warrior climbed up the tree and carefully hid himself in the branches. Then he waited to see what would take place.

Soon a young girl came to draw water from the well. She filled her jar with water and lifted it in both hands to place it on her head. Just then the young warrior plucked four or five of the willow leaves and let them flutter down. The leaves fell into the water which had just been drawn from the well. The young girl emptied the jar and drew fresh water from the well. The warrior again dropped leaves into the jar. Again the girl threw the leaves out and refilled her container. Once again the leaves came fluttering down, and once again the girl emptied the jar and refilled it.

"My, what a strong wind!" she said, and glanced up into the tree. At the sight of the warrior hidden there, she was startled. "Are you from the earth above? Why have you come to this place?" she asked.

The warrior then told her how the three princesses had been kidnapped by a giant eagle and how he had been sent to save them.

84

The girl suddenly started to cry and said, "To tell you the truth, I am the youngest of the three princesses who were seized by the eagle. I was brought here with my two sisters. I had given up all hope of ever returning home. You cannot imagine how happy I am to see you. The ogre has just gone out. Once he sets out he does not return for three months and ten days. But, if we run away now, it would mean that the ogre would still be living, and, as long as he lives, he will try to steal us away again. You must wait until the ogre comes back and then get rid of him for good. But can you do that?"

"Yes," the warrior answered, "of course, I can. That's why I came all this way."

"I'm glad to hear that," the princess answered.

"Come, I'll show you how to get into the ogre's house."

The youngest princess then led the young warrior to the ogre's house and hid him there in the storehouse. In the storehouse there was a large iron pestle. The princess pointed to it and said, "Let me see how strong you are. Try and lift that pestle."

The young warrior grabbed the iron pestle with both hands, but he couldn't budge the heavy pestle an inch.

"At that rate, you'll never be able to take the ogre's head," the princess said. She went into the ogre's house and returned with a bowl full of mandrake juice kept by the ogre, and told the young warrior to drink it. He drank the juice in one gulp, and when he grabbed the pestle again, he was able to move it just about an inch.

The young warrior stayed hidden in the storehouse. Every day he drank mandrake juice and wrestled with the iron pestle. Day after day he practiced and tested his strength. Finally, he was able to lift the iron pestle with one hand and fling it about as if it were a pair of chopsticks. But still the young warrior continued to drink the juice of the mandrake as he waited impatiently for the return of the ogre.

One day the ground began to tremble and the house to shake. The ogre had finally come home, together with his many henchmen. They brought with them many treasures which they had stolen. When they finished carrying everything into the house, they prepared a mighty banquet. That night, they feasted on delicacies of the mountains and the seas and drank wine by the barrel full. All night long they wined and danced, and the warrior watched them from the hidden place.

One by one the henchmen went to sleep, completely drunk. The ogre also finally toppled over in a drunken sleep. He lay snoring away.

"Now's my chance," the warrior thought and, drawing his sword, crept up to the sleeping ogre. But imagine the warrior's surprise! The ogre lay with his eyes wide open, although he was snoring loudly.

The princess, who had followed the young warrior into the room, then said in a small voice, "You don't have to worry. The ogre always sleeps with his eyes open."

Then with a tremendous shout, the warrior slashed with all his might at the ogre's neck. At this, the ogre jumped up, pulled out his sword, and tried to stop the blows. But the warrior's sharp blade had already bitten deep into the ogre's neck, and he could not move as quickly as usual. Under the strength of the warrior's repeated blows, the ogre finally toppled over again. The warrior sat on top of the huge giant and finally succeeded in cutting off his head.

The severed head, however bounded up and tried to attach itself to the bleeding neck. Just then the princess took out some fine ashes of burnt straw, which she had kept hidden under her dress, and threw them over the stump of the neck. The head let out one sad wail, then leaped up in one powerful jump, crashed through the ceiling, and disappeared.

The ogre's henchmen, when they learned what had happened to their chief, all surrendered meekly. The young warrior then threw open the many storehouses of the ogre, each filled to brimming with gold and silver, and divided up the treasure among the ogre's henchmen. Then he gathered together the three princesses and returned to the place where the basket had been lowered.

The warrior pulled at the rope, ringing the bell at the other end. The king's soldiers, who had been waiting there all this time, began hauling away. One by one the princesses were pulled up to the earth above. At the very end, the warrior also came up safely.

The king was so overjoyed at the return of his daughters that he ordered twenty-one days of celebration. The whole land also rejoiced that they were now safe from the terrors of the ogre from the Land-below-the-earth.

The king did not forget his promise to the young warrior. He gave his youngest daughter, the most beautiful of the three princesses, to the warrior in marriage. He also gave the young man much land and wealth. The young warrior and his beautiful wife lived long and happily ever after.

The Disowned Student

ong ago, there was once a young student. Now, it was the custom in those days for a student to go into the quiet of the mountains to some lonely temple and spend his days there studying in order to become a great scholar. So this young student left his home and went away to a mountain temple to read books and meditate for three long years. The days passed slowly at first. But one year passed, then two years, and in no time at all the three years were at an end. The student had completed his studies and could now go home to his parents.

However, whom should he see upon his return? There was another young student in his home, identical to himself in appearance, speech, and manner. What a surprise for the student to find someone just like himself! But what really troubled him was the fact that his own parents would not accept him as a member of the family. They treated him as if he were an imposter. He had come home after all these years, but they would not even let him enter the house.

"It's no joke," the young student said. "Can't you see I am your son? I've just returned from the temple after studying for three years. This young man must be an evil spirit." In this way the young student pleaded with his parents and his brothers and sisters to let him in the house.

The other student, however, did not remain silent. He shouted, "Be quiet, you imposter! You're just an old fox up to its trick of fooling people. Go away before we find you out."

That voice! It was the same as his own. It seemed impossible, yet even his own family could not tell the difference between the two. They looked the two boys over carefully. But the two students wore the same clothing. They even had the same birthmarks, the same scars. They were exactly alike. The parents then asked them about their birthdays and small details of their childhood and memories of any special occasion that might help solve the problem.

But the two boys gave the same answers. As a last resort, the parents then asked the two to name each article of furniture in the house, without leaving out an item.

Unfortunately, the real son had been away for three whole years, and he could not answer so easily. The other boy, however, had been living in the house for some time and was able to list everything without any trouble.

"Well, that decides it," the family said. "You are the imposter. Be on your way!" So saying, they finally drove their real son out of the house.

The poor young man did not know what to do. He knew it was useless to argue, so he left. Day after day he wandered lonely here and there.

One day, he met a priest who gazed kindly into his face and said, "You've had yourself stolen, haven't you? There is someone who looks exactly like you, isn't there? Someone who has taken your place?"

"Here's someone who may be able to help me," thought the young man, surprised at the way the priest could read his troubles. So the young man opened up his heart and told the priest how he had returned home after three years of study only to find that someone else had taken his place in his home. He also told the priest how he had been chased out by his family.

"H'm, h'm," the priest nodded, as he listened to this tale. "Did you ever throw away the clippings of your fingernails somewhere while you were studying at the temple?"

"Yes," the student answered, "there was a river running right in front of the temple. I used to bathe in that river. Then after bathing, I would sit on the stones nearby and cut my nails. The clippings I left on the stony river bank."

"Just as I thought," the priest said. "Whoever has eaten your fingernail clippings has taken over your identity. Go straight home once again. But this time take a cat with you. Hide it in the sleeve of your robe so that no one will know that you have it. When you get home, let the cat out right in front of the imposter. Then all will become known."

The student did as the priest told him and returned home. His parents came out again. So did the imposter. But before they could say anything, the young student let the cat out from his sleeve, right in front of the person who had taken his place in the family.

The imposter suddenly turned white, and the cat pounced upon him and bit him on the neck. There was a great struggle. In the end, the imposter fell to the ground, right in the middle of the room, his throat cut open by the cat's sharp teeth. The parents and the brothers and sisters looked carefully. There, to their surprise, lay not their son and brother, but a large field rat!

The rat had eaten the clippings of the young student's fingernails and had stolen his identity. The spirit of human beings dwells in the fingernails. Thus, the rat who ate the student's fingernail clippings had been able to change readily into the shape of the young man. But a cat can smell a rat, no matter how disguised. And so, thanks to the priest's wise advice, the story ends happily.

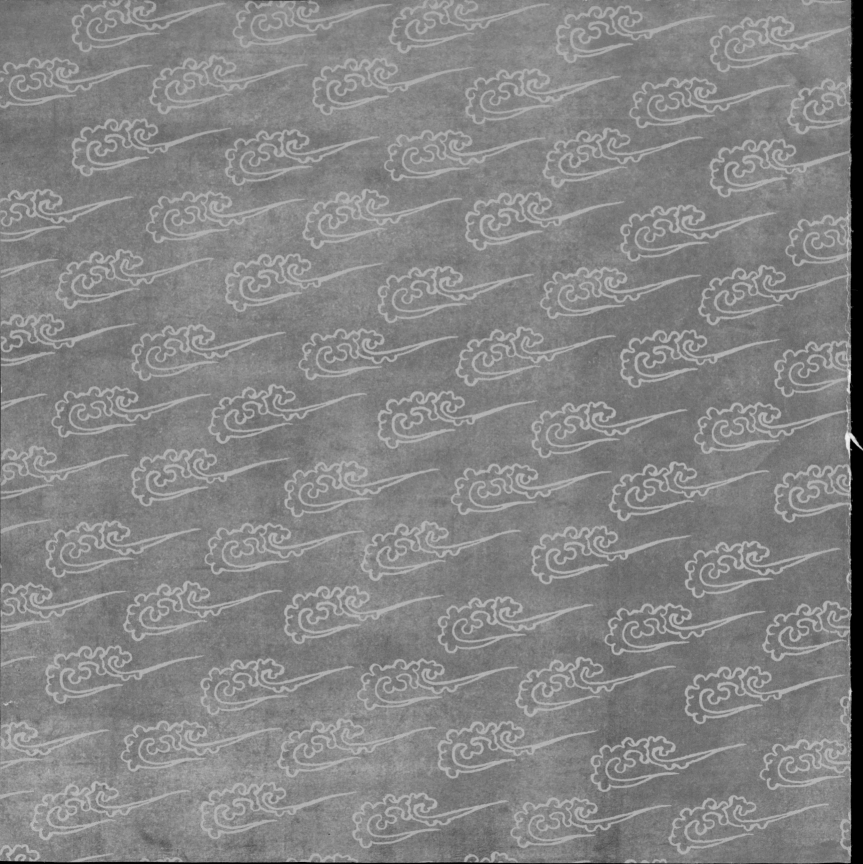